TEAM STRINGS

Viola

CHRISTOPHER BULL
OLIVE GOODBORN
& RICHARD DUCKETT

Edited by Barrie Carson Turner

First published in 1993 by International Music Publications Ltd
This edition © 2014 by Faber Music Ltd
This edition first published in 2014 by Faber Music Ltd
Bloomsbury House
74–77 Great Russell Street
London WC1B 3DA
Cover photography by Keven Erickson
Cover design by Susan Clarke
Instruments photographed by kind permission of Yamaha-Kemble Music (UK) Ltd
Typeset by Cromwell Typesetting & Design Ltd, London
Printed in England by Caligraving Ltd
All rights reserved

ISBN10: 0-571-52801-5
EAN13: 978-0-571-52801-1

To buy Faber Music publications or to find out about the full range of titles
available please contact your local music retailer or Faber Music sales enquiries:

Faber Music Ltd, Burnt Mill, Elizabeth Way, Harlow CM20 2HX
Tel: +44 (0) 1279 82 89 82
fabermusic.com

Introduction

The *Team Strings* series has been designed to meet the needs of young string players everywhere, whether lessons are given individually, in groups or in the classroom.

Musical variety

Each book contains a wide variety of musical styles, from the Baroque and Classical eras to Christmas carols, folk music and popular favourites. In addition there are many original pieces and studies, technical exercises and scales. Furthermore *Team Strings* offers material for mixed string ensemble as well as solos with piano accompaniment.

Audio

 The accompanying downloadable audion contains over 80 digital backing tracks for individual and group use. To download it scan the QR code or go to fabermusic.com/audio. See page iv for a complete track listing.

General musicianship skills

In addition to fostering literacy, *Rhythm Grids* and *Play by Ear* lines provide early opportunities for composition and improvisation. Comprehensive notes on the use of this series, scores of ensemble pieces, piano accompaniments and approaches to creative music making are given in the *Team Strings Piano Accompaniment* book (0-571-52804-X).

Acknowledgements

Sincere thanks are extended to Ann Goodborn, double bass tutor, for her invaluable advice on technical matters, Angela Gregory, and all the pupils who worked on the material in preparation.

Copyright acknowledgements

Team Strings ensemble

The ensemble material in *Team Strings* has been specially written so that it can be played by almost any combination of string instruments: there are a wide range of ensemble options to experiment with which are explained below. *Team Strings* can also be integrated with *Team Brass* and *Team Woodwind*, which will enable you to use the pieces in a classroom setting. Much of the *Team* ensemble material now plays a prominent part in the Music Medals syllabus of the ABRSM.

Ensemble pieces within *Team Strings*

☐ These pieces appear in the same place on the same page in all four *Team Strings* books and can be played together in unison. Thus, even beginners are given early ensemble experience and the opportunity to share lessons with other players.

Ensemble pieces marked with this logo can be expanded into almost any combination of string instruments playing together in harmony. Scores of this ensemble material are given in the *Team Strings Piano Accompaniment* book (0-571-52804-X). These pieces can also be expanded to include woodwind and brass instruments (see below).

Integrating the viola with *Team Woodwind* and *Team Brass*

The *Team Strings Viola Supplement* for Team Woodwind (flute and oboe) is available for free download from fabermusic.com, allowing the viola to play with the duets in the *Team Flute* and *Team Oboe* books. Some of these pieces can also be used in conjunction with selected pieces in *Team Brass* (see supplement for full details).

Integrating brass and woodwind players with *Team Strings*

Supplements are also available for free download from fabermusic.com for brass and woodwind players to join in with the *Team Strings* ensemble pieces. Each ensemble piece can therefore be extended to incorporate a wide variety of additional instruments. These supplementary parts can be used for almost any combination of instruments up to full orchestra.

Piano accompaniments

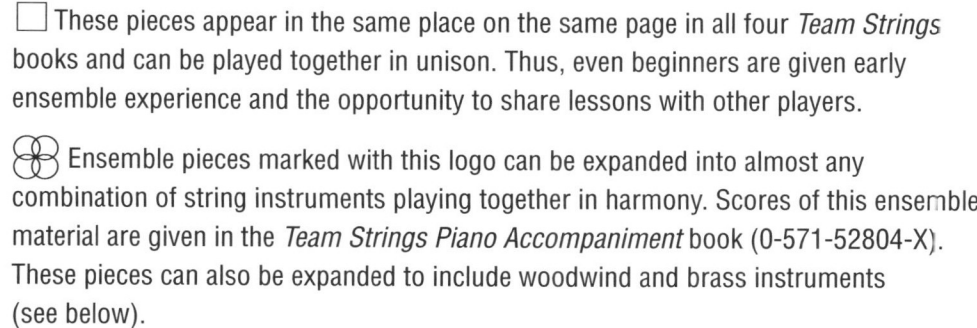 This logo indicates which pieces have a piano accompaniment. In order to help young string players with intonation, the tune is included in the piano accompaniment. Scores for all ensemble material and more extensive notes are also included in the *Team Strings Piano Accompaniment* book (0-571-52804-X).

Audio track listing

Some tracks work with two different tunes.
Each track includes two bars of clicks to bring you in.

Audio orchestrated by Gordon Watts
Production: Mark Mumford
Track 16 published by EMI United Partnership Ltd.
Track 17 published by Peter Maurice Music Co. Ltd.
Track 21 published by Williamson Music Co.
Track 32 published by Keith Prowse Music Pub. Co. Ltd.
Track 82 published by B Feldman Corp.
All other tracks ℗ and © 1994 International Music Publications Ltd.

Lesson diary & practice chart

Date (week commencing)	Enter number of minutes practised.							Teacher indicates which pages to study.
	Mon	Tue	Wed	Thur	Fri	Sat	Sun	

Start with D . . .

2

*French time-names may be used.

. . . then on to A

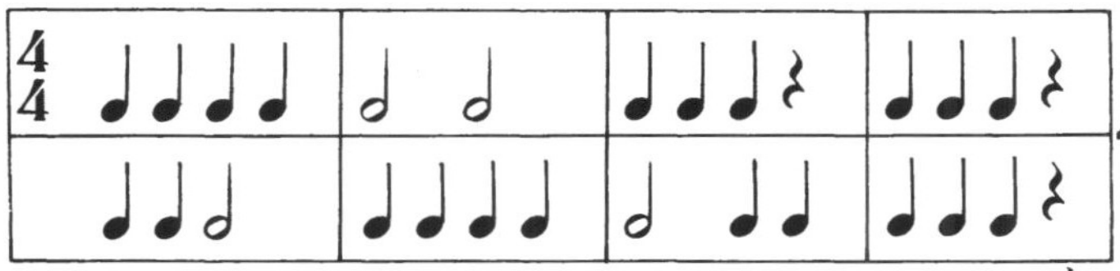

Clap, say, and play the rhythm

A CROTCHET REST lasts for ONE beat

Open A is written above the top line

BAR LINES divide a line of notes into sets. In $\frac{4}{4}$ time each bar adds up to four crotchet beats

1+1+1+1= 4

2+2= 4

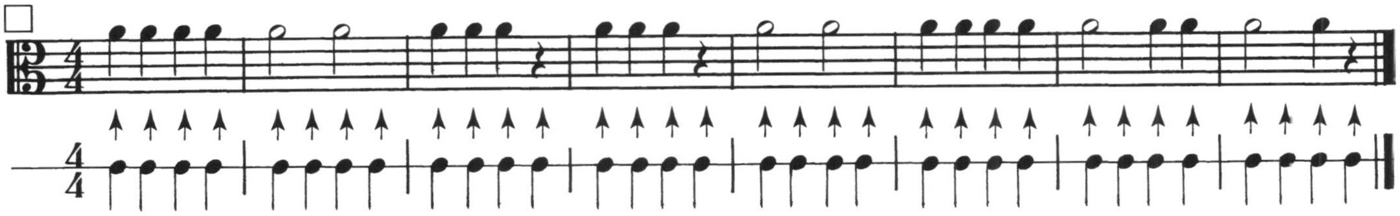

D and A together

A MINIM rest lasts for two beats

Find the A string with your finger during the rests

Music is written on a set of five lines and four spaces called a STAVE

By the Rhine

This piece fits with *German tune* (page 23).

The note G

Music for the viola begins with the ALTO CLEF

Open G is written in the bottom space

G and D together

A little march

Chiming bells

G, D and A

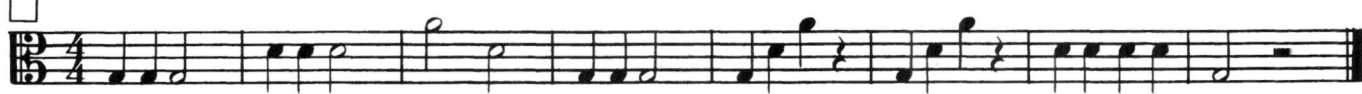

The note C

On the lake

This piece fits with *Flamingo* (page 12).

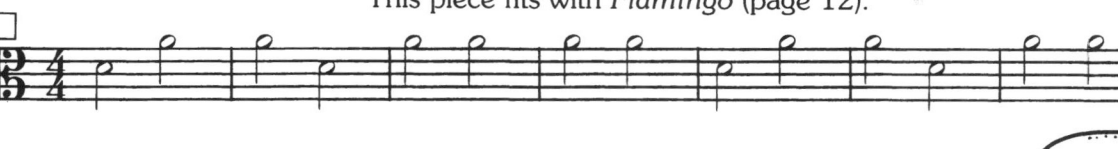

The DOUBLE BAR marks the end of a piece of music

The traveller

This piece fits with *Tramping* (page 11).

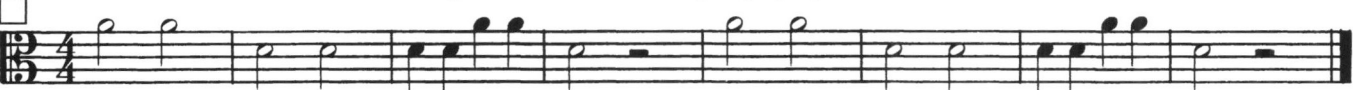

The pendulum

This piece fits with *The clock* (page 15).

At dusk

This piece fits with *Now the day is over* (page 19).

Magic spells

This piece fits with *The wizard* (page 43).

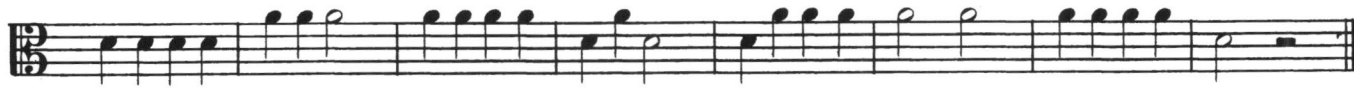

Down bow

Using the bow

Up bow

ARCO means play with the bow.

PIZZICATO (or *pizz*) means pluck the strings.

From now on everything can be played *arco*, unless marked otherwise.

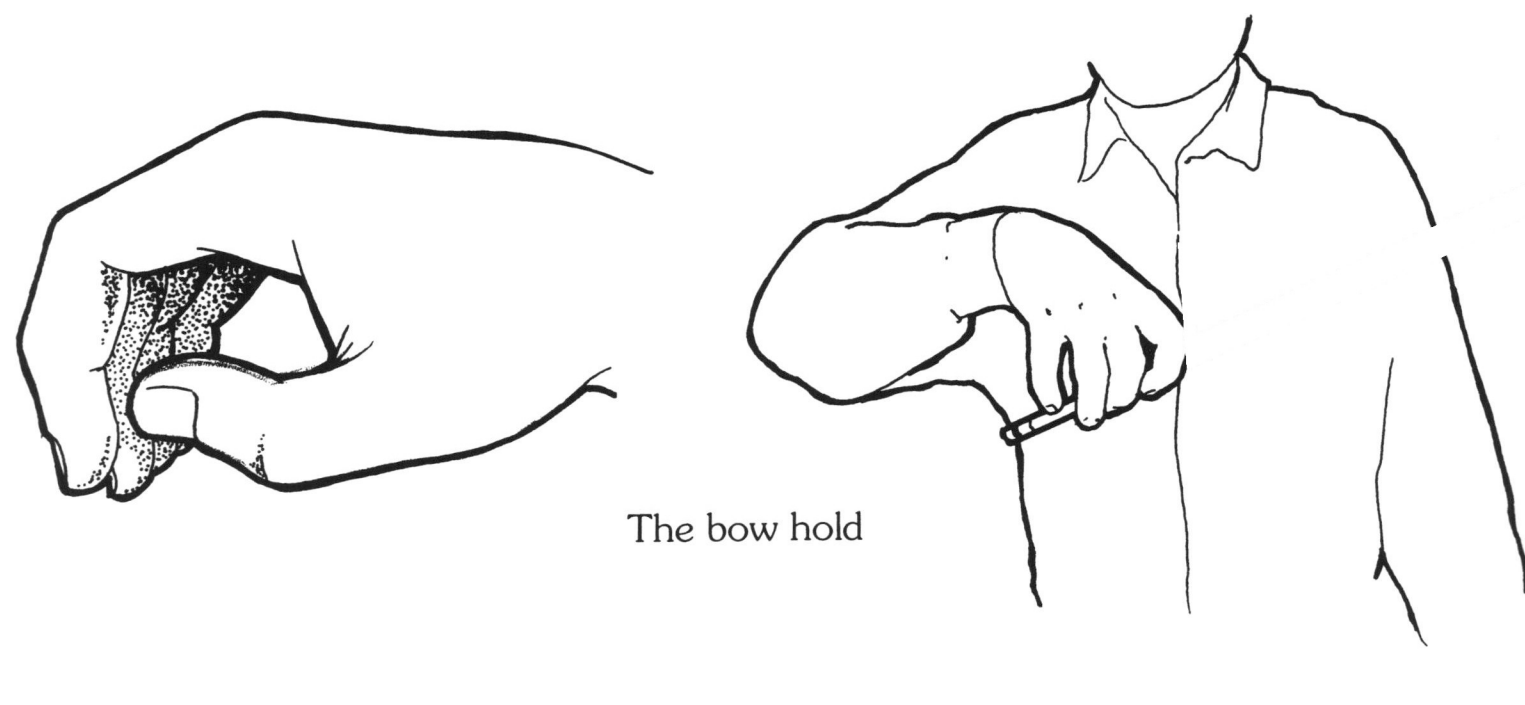

The bow hold

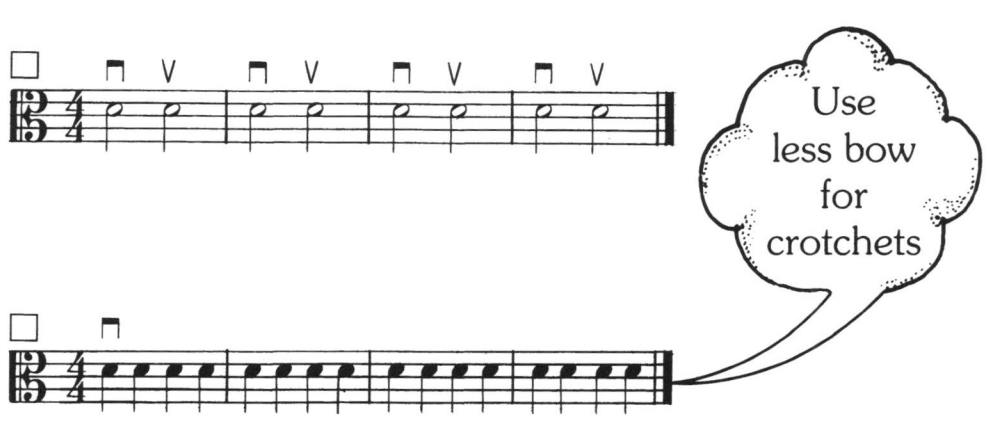

Use less bow for crotchets

Bowing exercises

Watch out for these signs

Always keep your bow straight!

■ The music on pages 2 - 7 can also be used as bowing exercises.

First finger E

This E is written on the fourth line

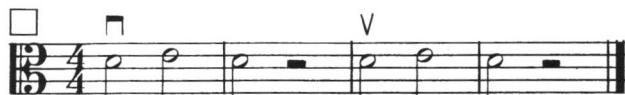

By the stream

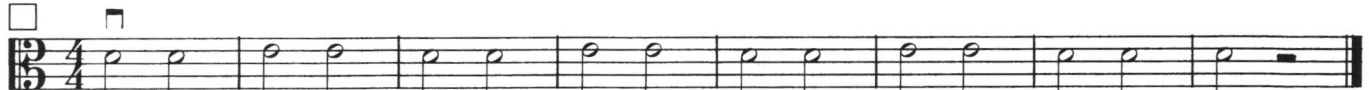

The night sky

This piece fits with *Twinkle, twinkle little star* (page 27).

Second finger F♯

This F sharp is written in the top space

Tramping

Down bow

Traditional

The sharp sign makes all the notes in the bar with the same letter name sharp

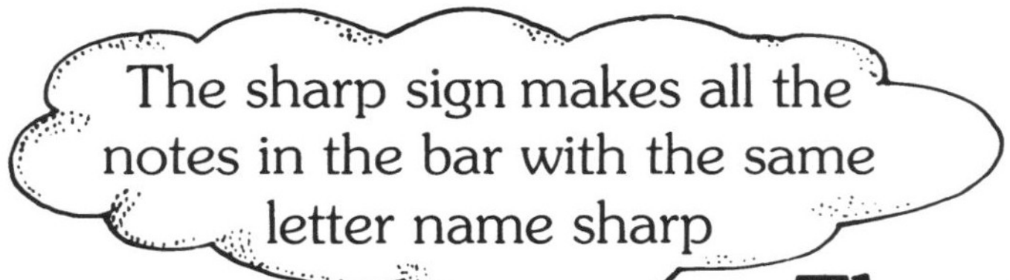

The shepherd

Bavaria

This piece fits with *German tune* (page 23).

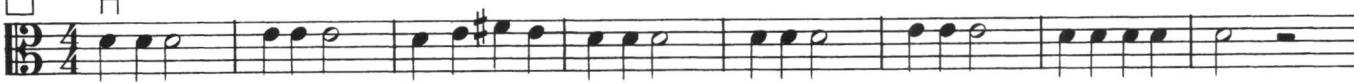

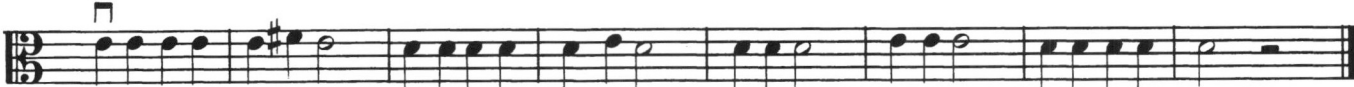

Third finger G

This G is written on the top line

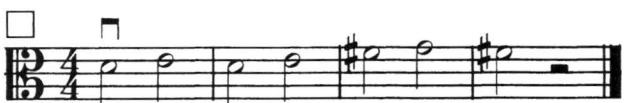

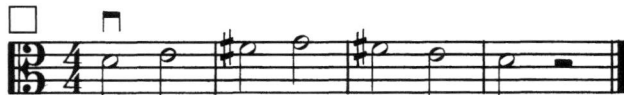

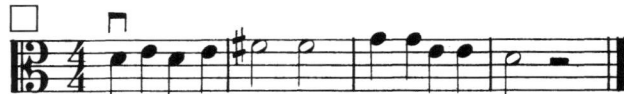

Flamingo

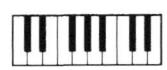

The magic carpet

This piece fits with *The wizard* (page 43).

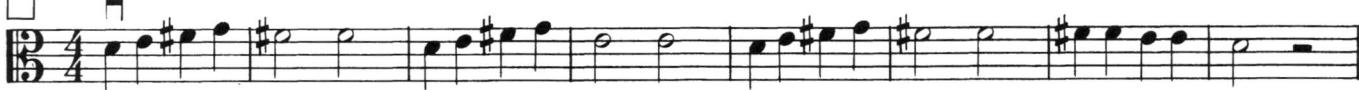

Tunes using D E F♯ & G

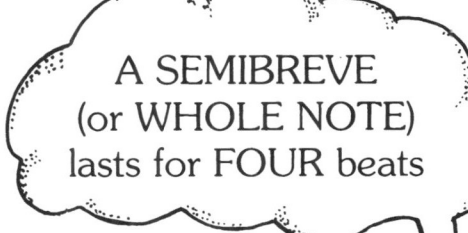

A SEMIBREVE
(or WHOLE NOTE)
lasts for FOUR beats

The piper

Lucy

Folk song

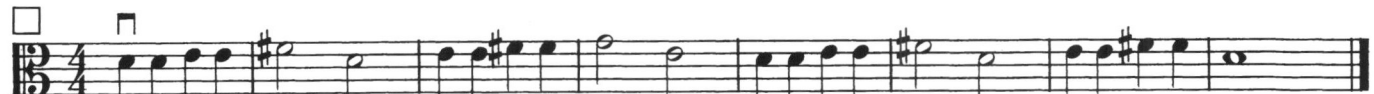

Falling leaves

This piece fits with *Autumn* (page 21).

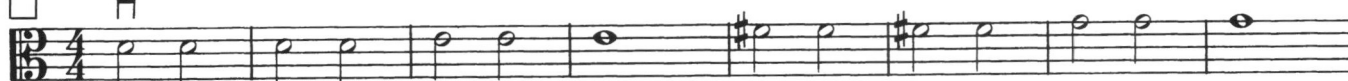

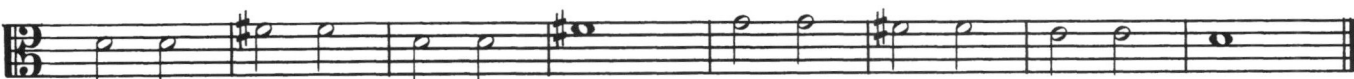

Gospel song

This piece fits with *All night, all day* (page 51).

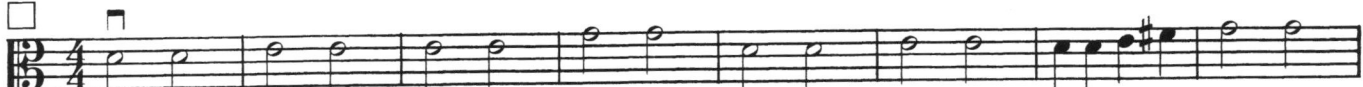

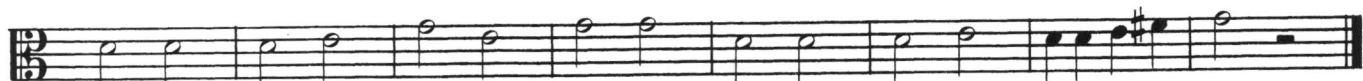

Kingston

This piece fits with *Jamaican dance* (page 49).

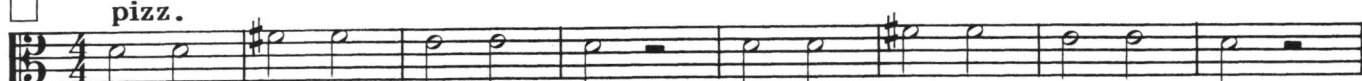

Coronation march

This piece fits with *Procession* (page 25).

The astronomer

This piece fits with *Twinkle, twinkle little star* (page 27).

Notes on the G string

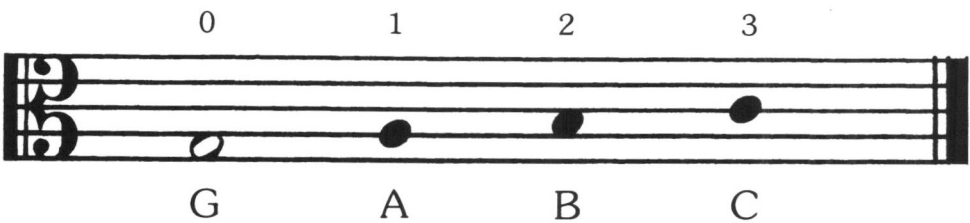

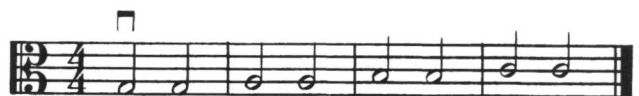

Merrily we roll along

Traditional

On parade

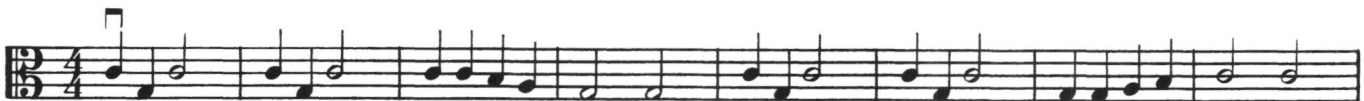

The clock

In the belfry

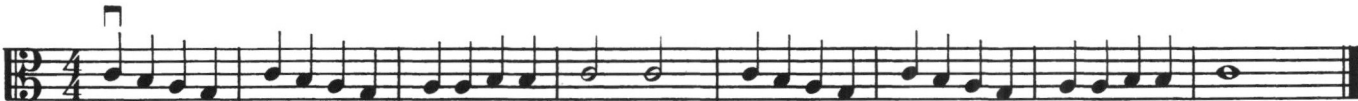

Pennyroyal

Chorale

Scottish air

Rutland

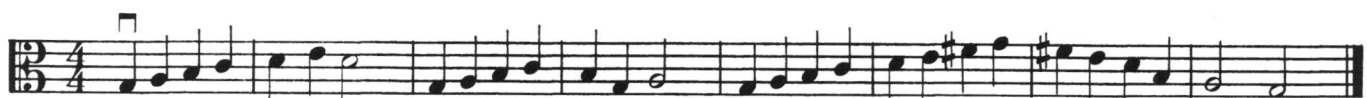

The grasshopper

Notes on the A string

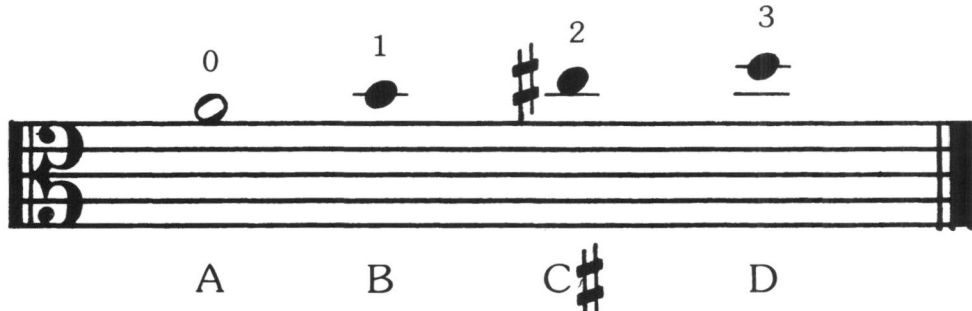

The harvest

Au clair de la lune

French traditional

> Make up your own piece using the notes on the A string

Dance

The key signature of G

The key signature of D

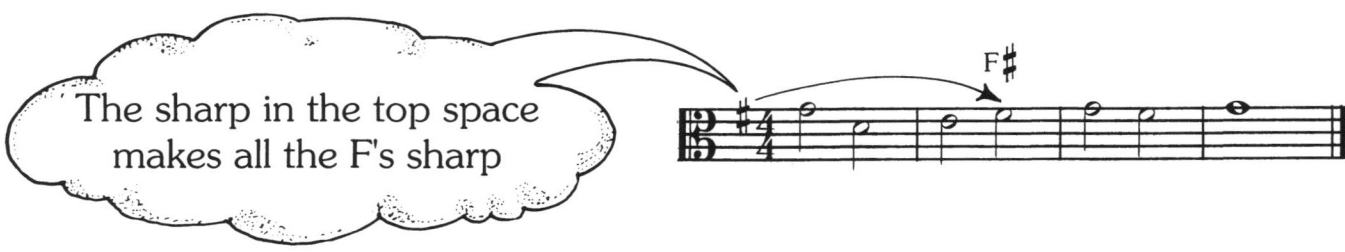

The sharp in the top space makes all the F's sharp

Promenade

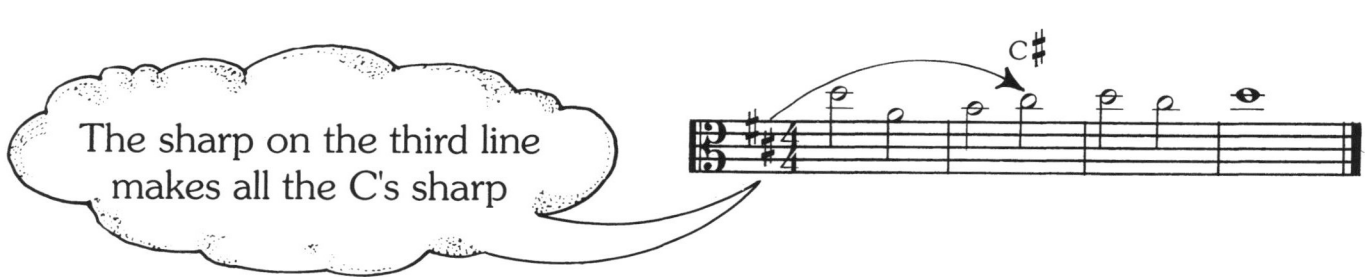

The sharp on the third line makes all the C's sharp

Daydreams

Five-note patterns

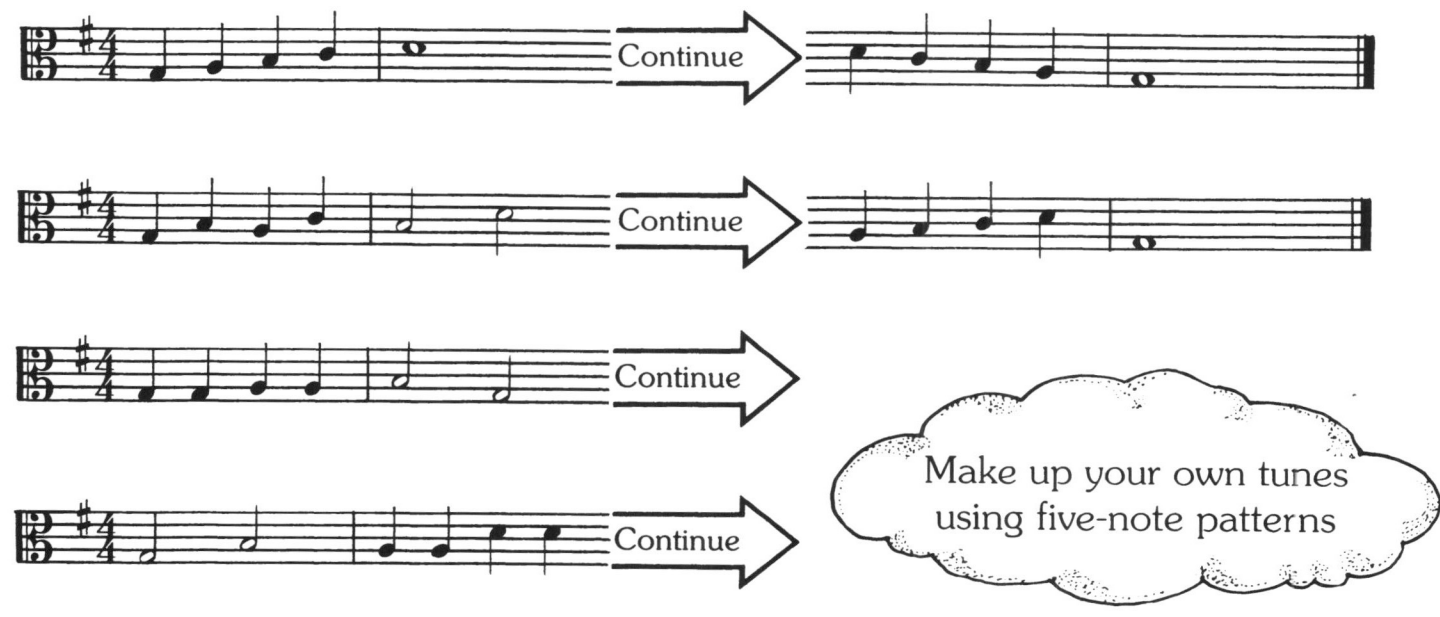

Now the day is over

S. BARING-GOULD (1834-1924)

Quick march

Mr Foster's round

Chinese lantern

Poor Tom

Duet

Autumn

Dotted minims

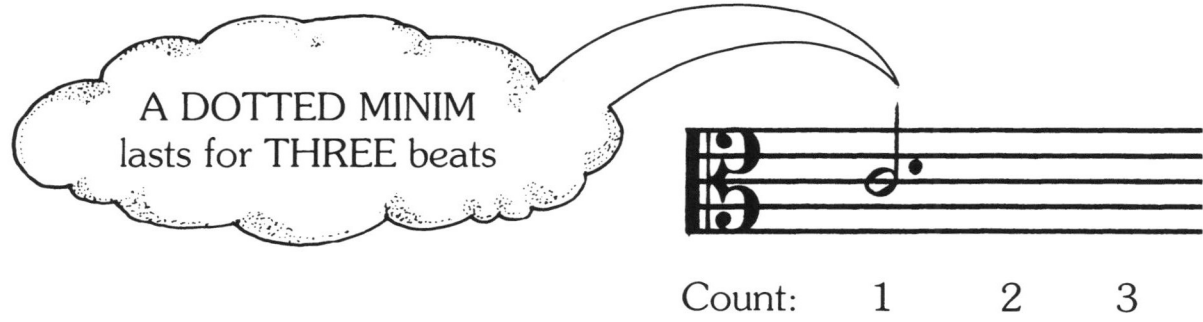

A DOTTED MINIM lasts for THREE beats

Count: 1   2   3

Sorrow

Rigaudon

HENRY PURCELL (1658-1695)

Arpeggios

Shady grove

American traditional

German tune

Traditional

Quavers

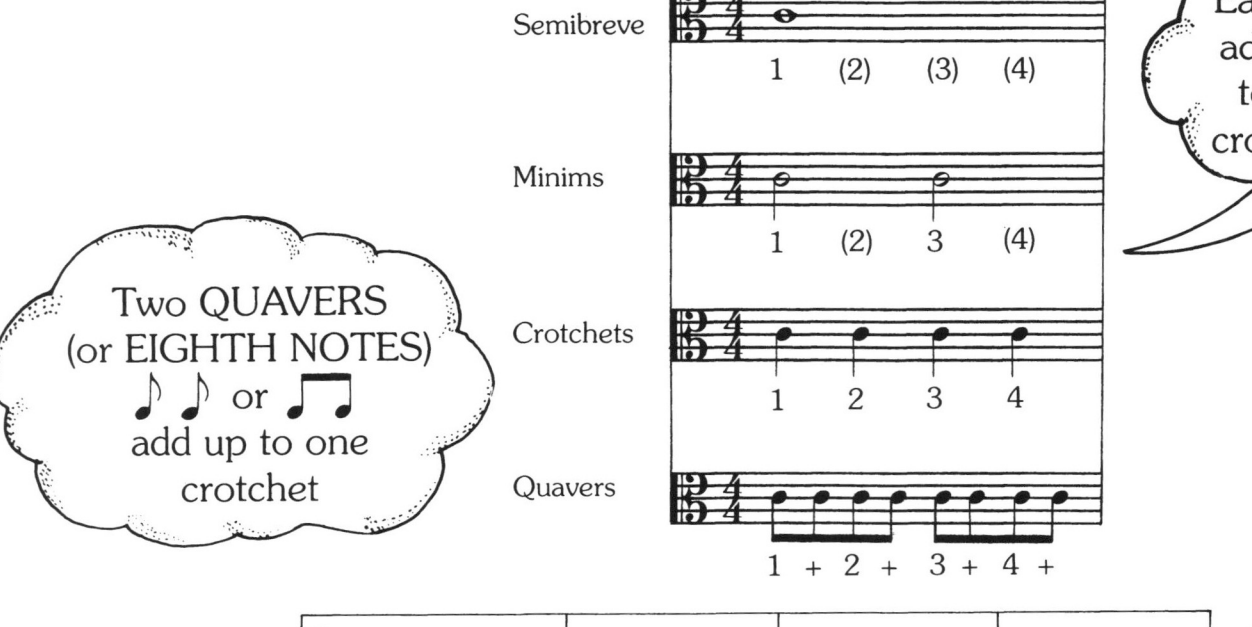

Each bar adds up to four crotchets

Two QUAVERS (or EIGHTH NOTES) ♪♪ or ♫ add up to one crotchet

Clap, say, and play the rhythm

My goose

Round

Who's that yonder?

The two dots mean that the music should be repeated

Spiritual

Procession

1.

2.

3.

This old man

English traditional

Round go the mill wheels

French traditional

Song and dance

West Indian traditional

One player only

Everyone together

Solo

Tutti

Solo

Tutti

Solo

Tutti

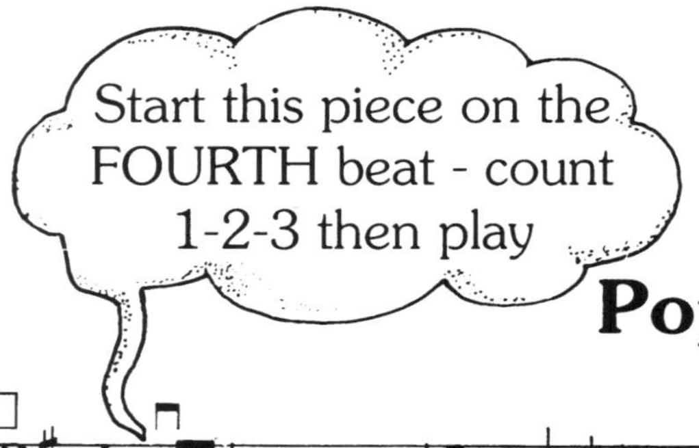

Solo

Tutti

Start this piece on the FOURTH beat - count 1-2-3 then play

Popular song

American traditional

Twinkle, twinkle little star

Traditional

'Swops'

Duet

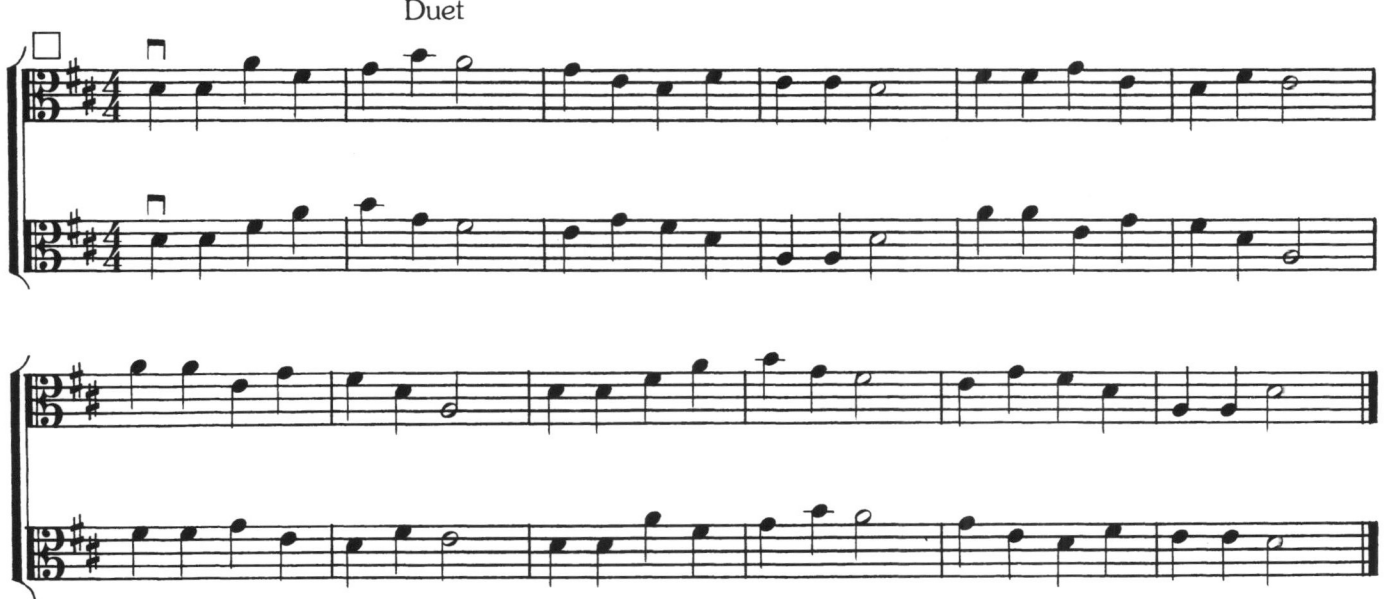

Little donkey

Words and Music by
ERIC BOSWELL

Okushiri

Japanese traditional

In $\frac{2}{4}$ time
each bar adds up
to TWO beats

Kol dodi

Jewish traditional

Russian lullaby

Go tell Aunt Rhody

American traditional

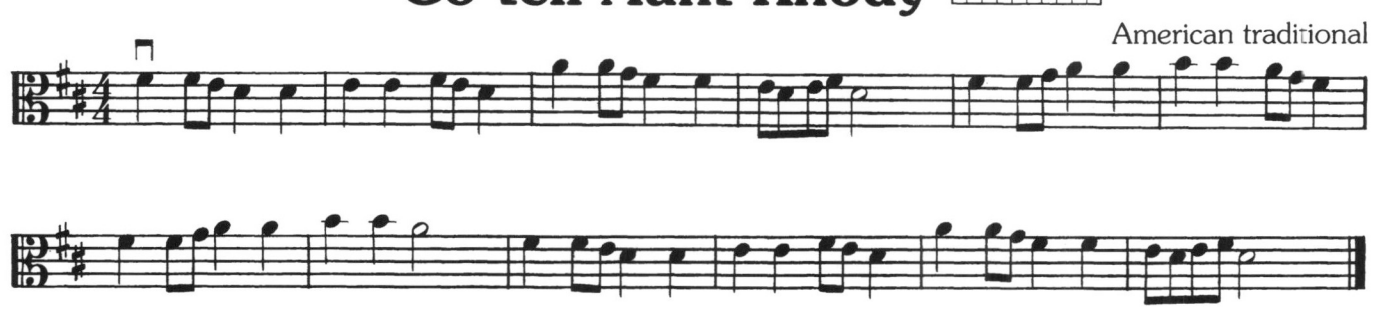

Magnolia

Long, long ago  T. H. BAYLY

Composing your own music

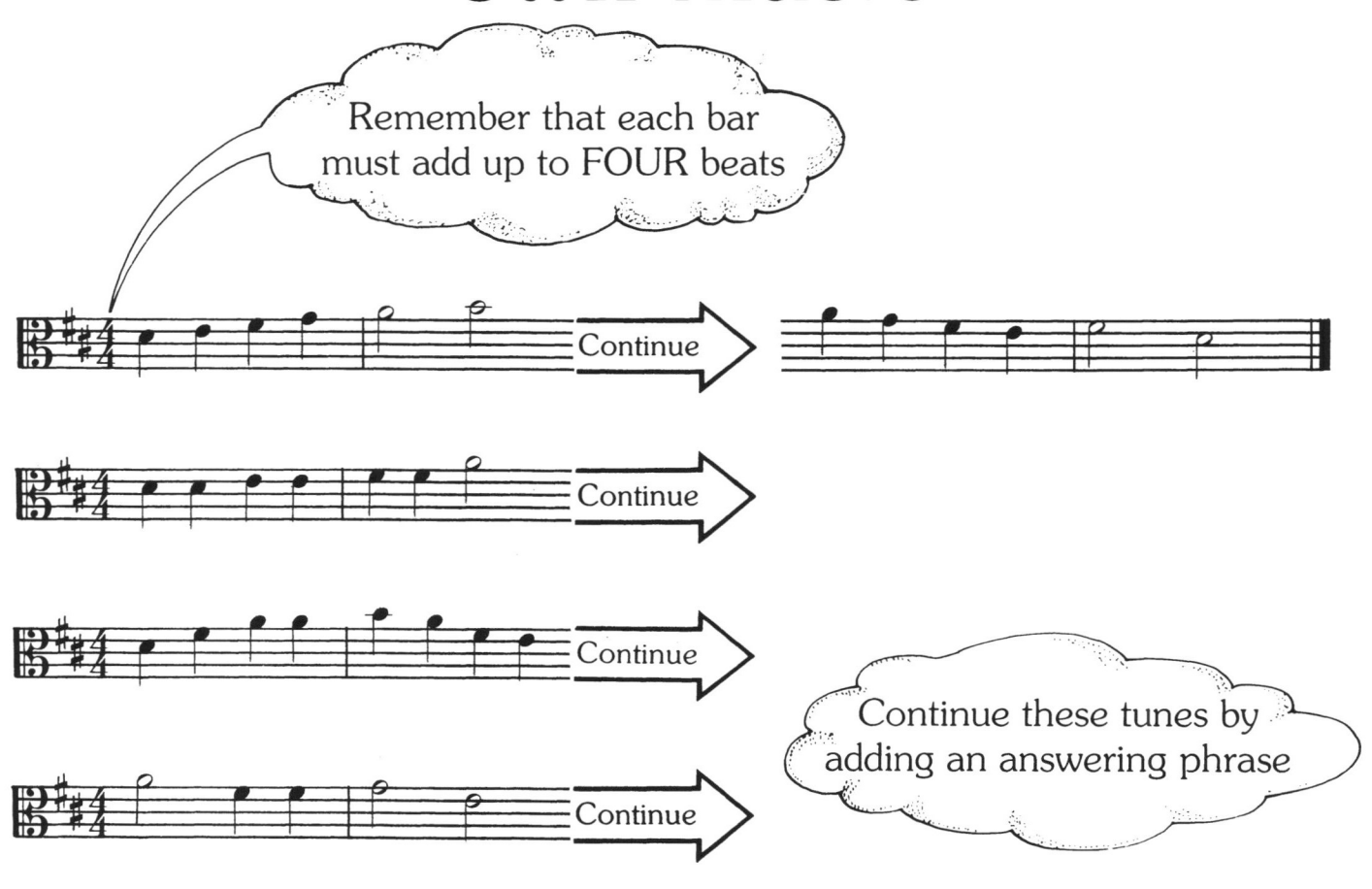

Round

Workin' on the railroad

Notes on the C string

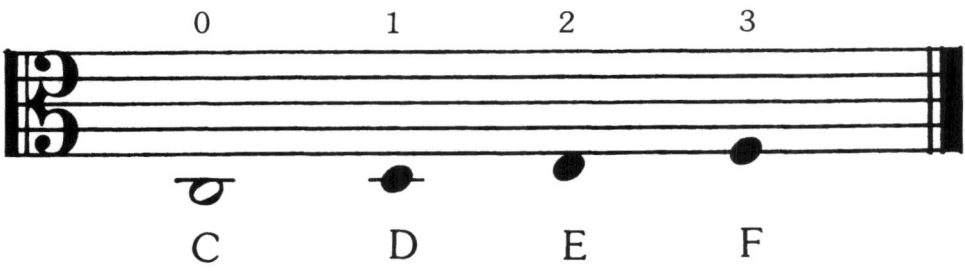

Cowboy song

Ozibani

Tribal song from Zambia

Welcome spring

Swiss traditional

Hide and seek

German traditional

$\frac{3}{4}$ time

Each bar adds up to three crotchet beats

Waltz

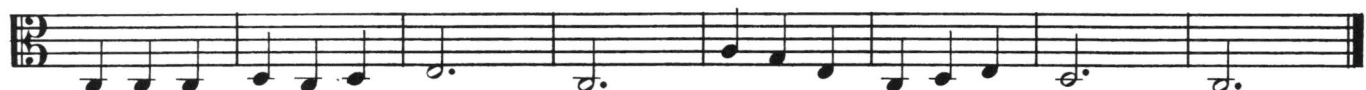

Going home

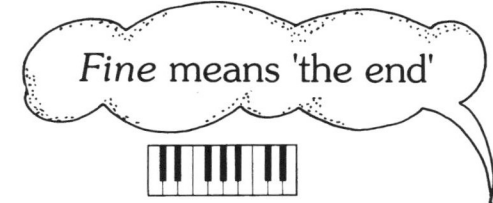

Fine means 'the end'

Go back to the beginning and finish at the bar marked *Fine*

Blow the wind southerly

English traditional

Chanson

Eliza

Fine

D.%. al Fine

Go back to the sign ·%· and
play through to the word *Fine*

Past three o'clock

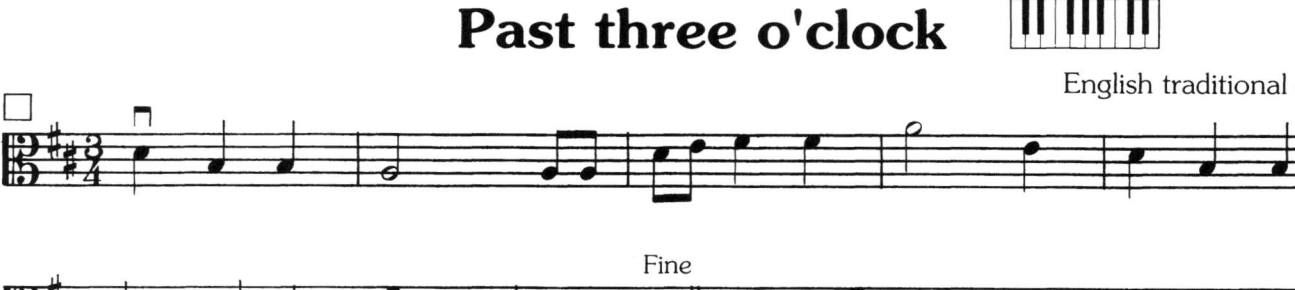

English traditional carol

Fine

D.C. al Fine

Oranges and lemons

English traditional

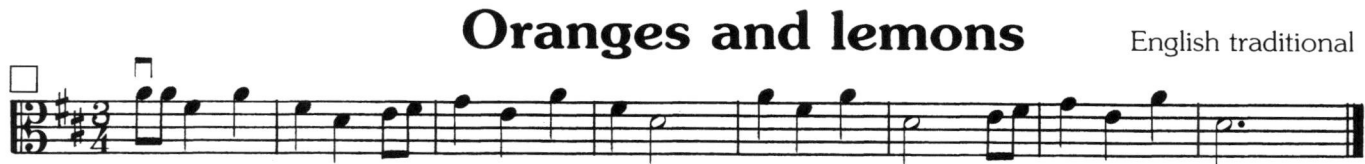

London's burning

Round

English traditional

(1) (2) (3) (4)

Ye banks and braes

Scottish traditional

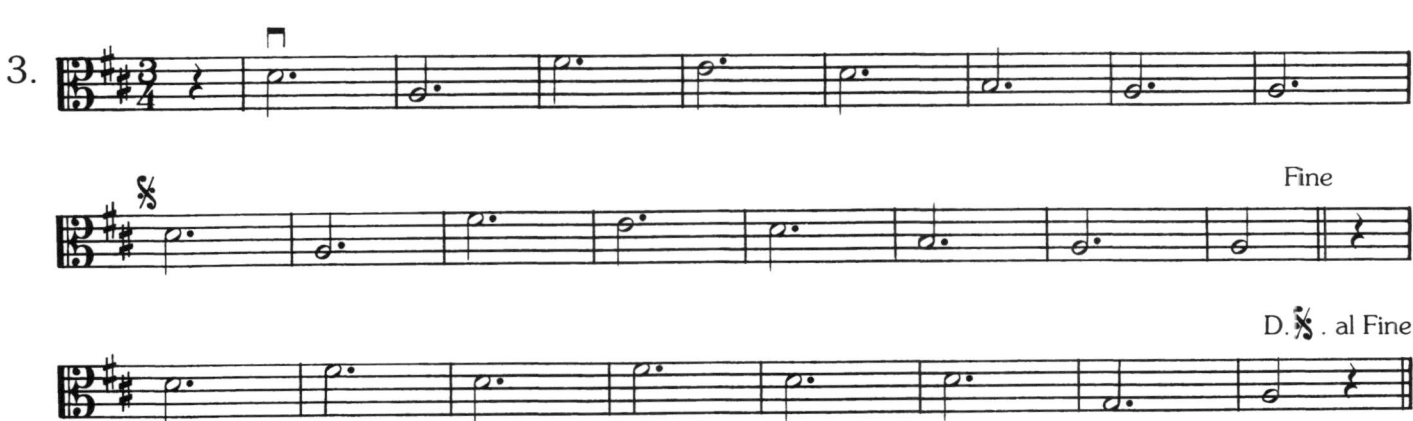

A handsome lad

QUAVER rest

Irish traditional

Lively

Congratulations

Up bow

Happily

Words and Music by
BILL MARTIN and PHIL COULTER

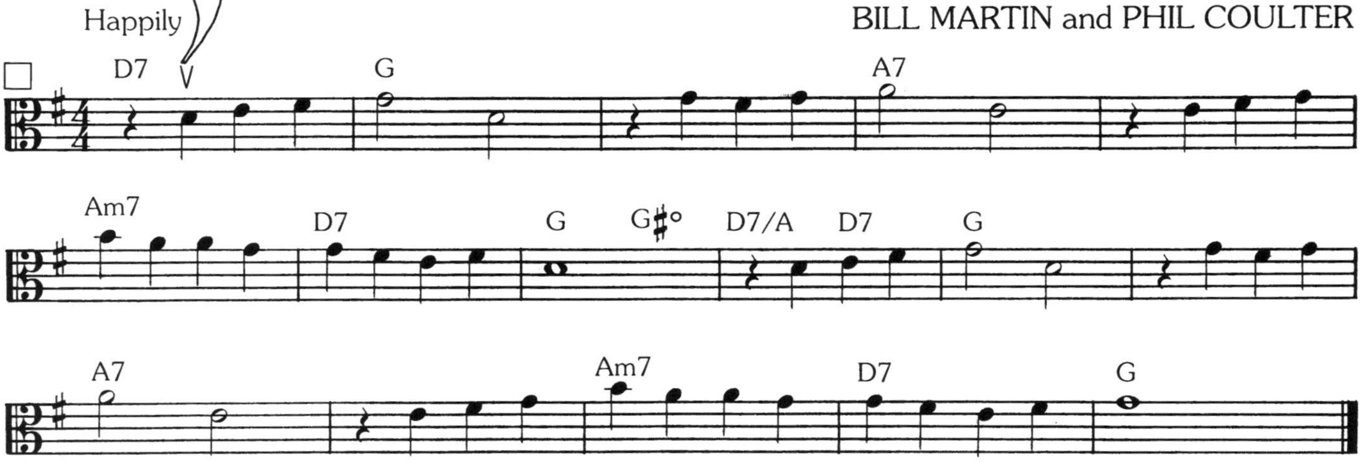

Minuet

WOLFGANG AMADEUS MOZART
(1756-1791)

Moderately

Mongoose

Brightly

Jamaican traditional

The prospector

Up bow

Steadily

American traditional

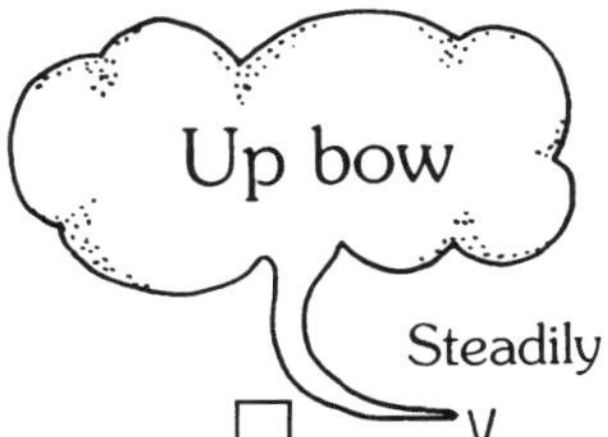

Schottisch

FRANZ SCHUBERT
(1797-1828)

Simply

Now we are met

Slowly   Duet

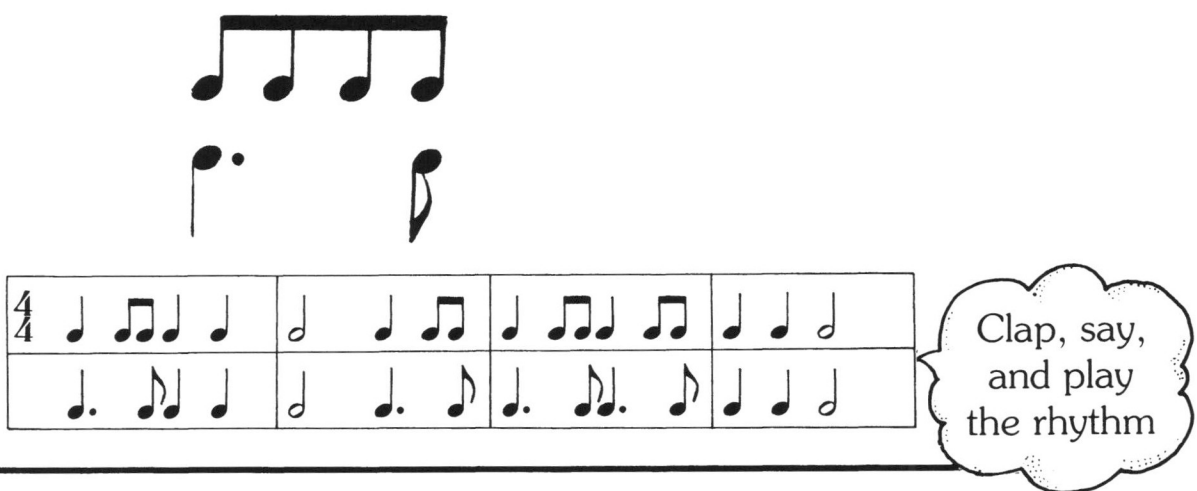

Dotted crotchets

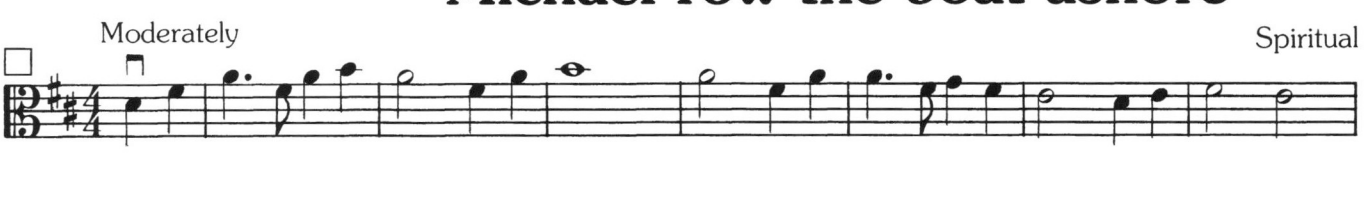

Michael row the boat ashore

Moderately — Spiritual

The muffin man

English traditional

Rhythmically

Village song

Not too fast — Peruvian traditional

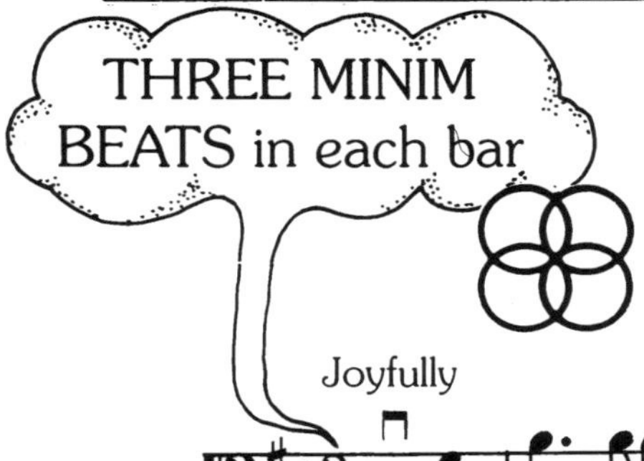

THREE MINIM BEATS in each bar

Kum ba yah

Spiritual

Joyfully

1.

Joyfully

2.

Joyfully

3.

Edelweiss
From *The Sound of Music*

Lyrics by OSCAR HAMMERSTEIN II
Music by RICHARD RODGERS

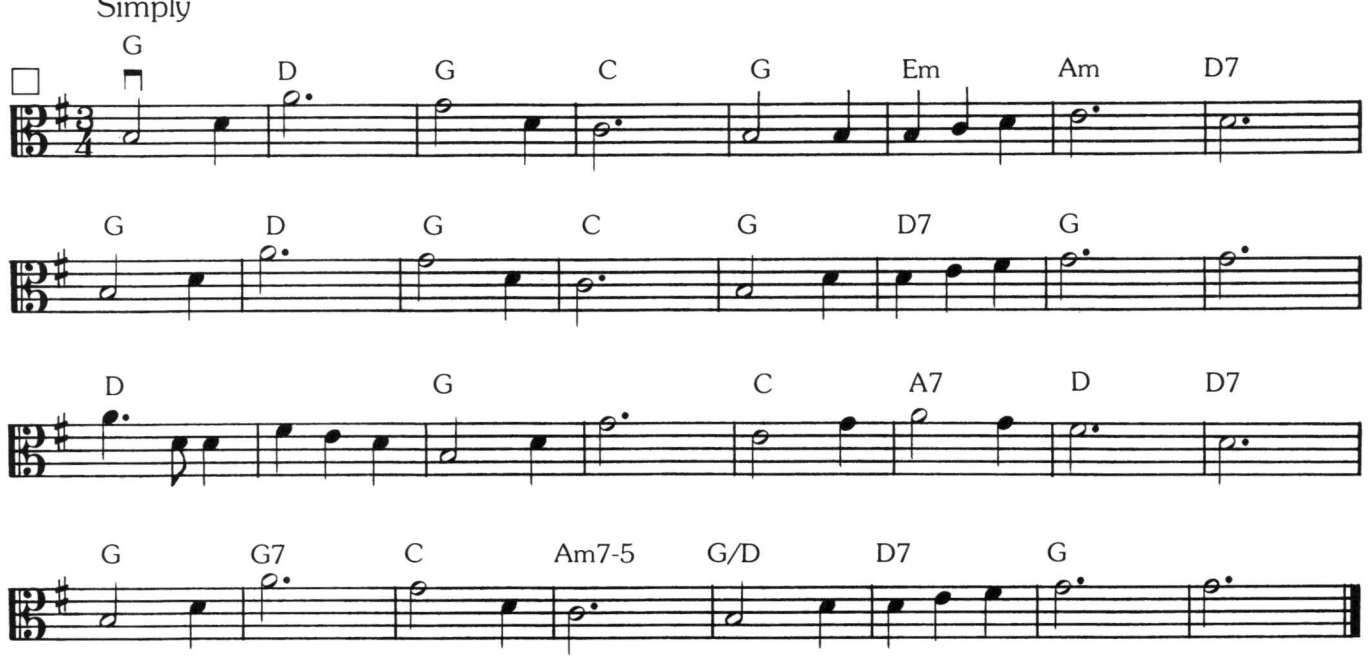

London bridge

English traditional

Donkey riding

Traditional

Music for viols

Anon (16th Century)

Paloma blanca

Words and Music by
J BOUWENS

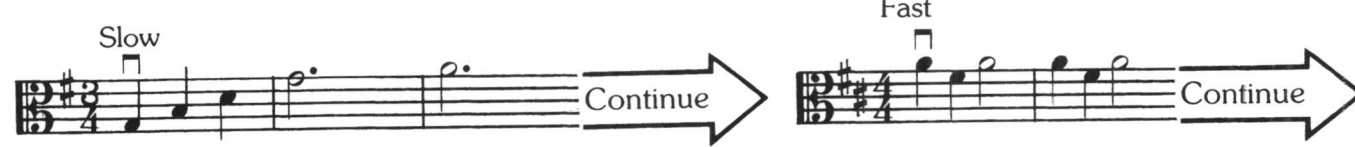

Slurs

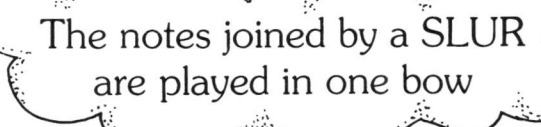

The notes joined by a SLUR
are played in one bow

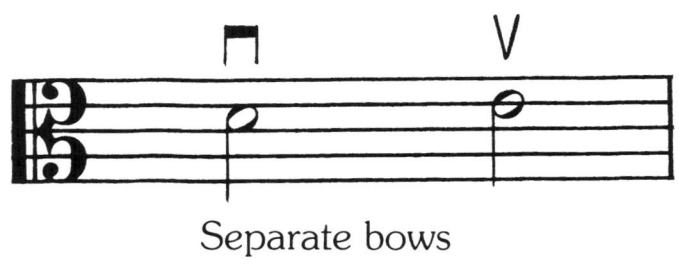

Separate bows

Slur

Scale of G

Etude

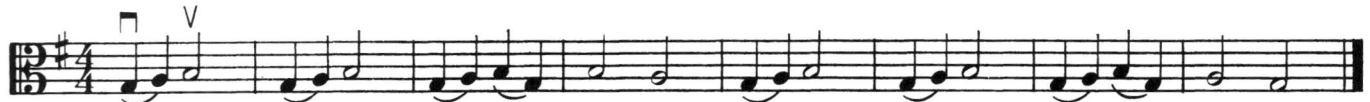

Ode to joy

From the Ninth Symphony

LUDWIG VAN BEETHOVEN
(1770-1827)

Majestically

The wizard

1st and 2nd-time bars

The nightingale

On the repeat, omit these bars and go straight to the bar marked 2

Bonjour!

Composed by twelve-year old Bernadette Walker

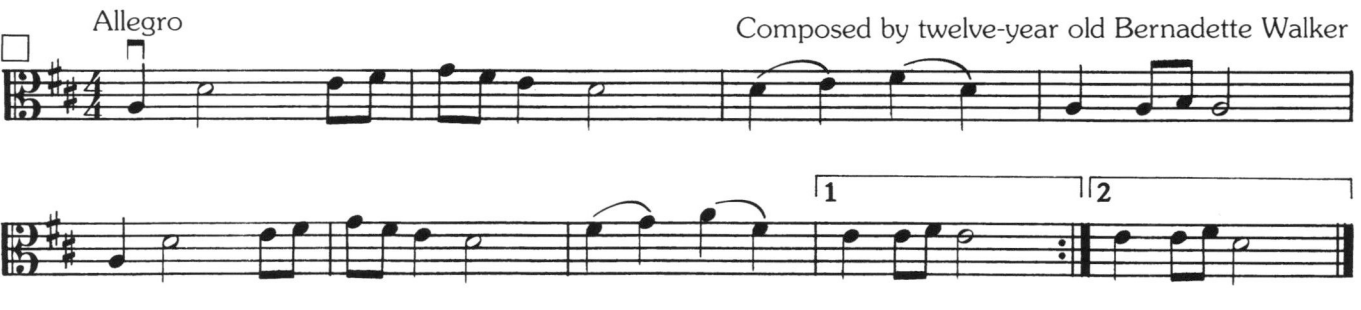

Allegro

TIELMAN SUSATO (c.16th)

Jingle bells

Presto

American traditional

The first Nowell

Joyfully

English traditional carol

O come, all ye faithful

Moderato

(Accompaniment)

J.F. WADE (1711-1786)

O little town of Bethlehem

Moderato

(Accompaniment)

English traditional carol

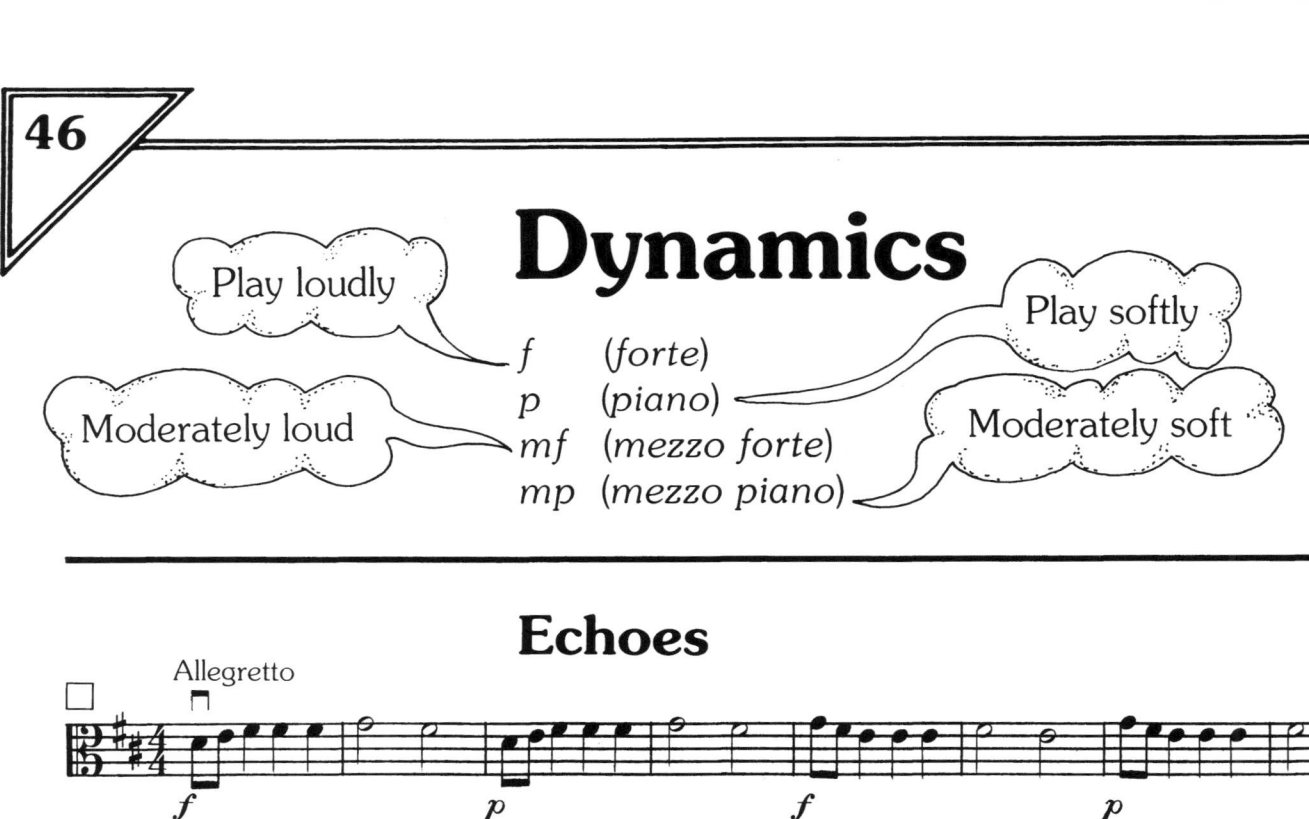

Dynamics

Play loudly	
Moderately loud	*f* (forte)
	p (piano) — **Play softly**
	mf (mezzo forte) — **Moderately soft**
	mp (mezzo piano)

Echoes

Allegretto

f   *p*   *f*   *p*

f   *p*   *f*   *p*

Frère Jacques

French traditional

Brightly   Round

(1)   (2)   (3)   (4)

f   *p*   *f*   *p*   *f*   *p*   *f*   *p*

The willow tree

Flowing

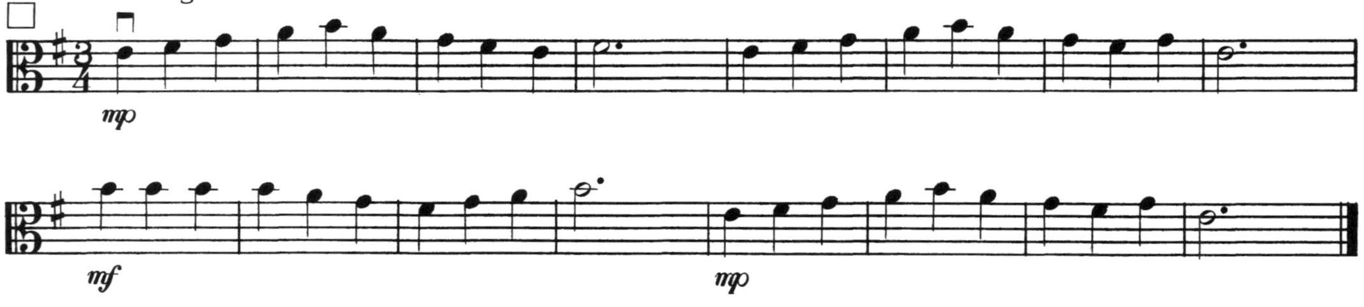

mp

mf   *mp*

Pattern

Moderato

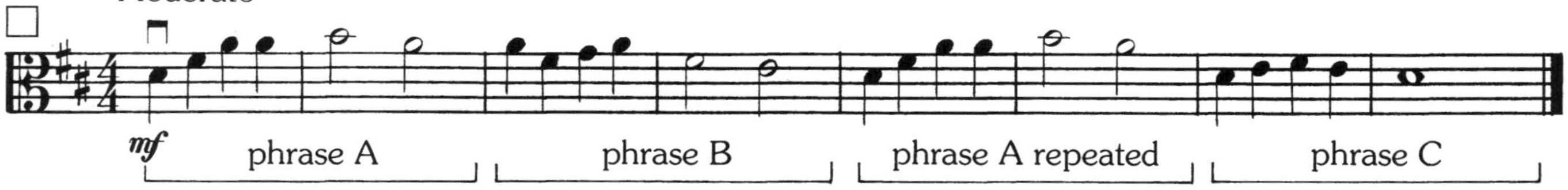

mf   phrase A   phrase B   phrase A repeated   phrase C

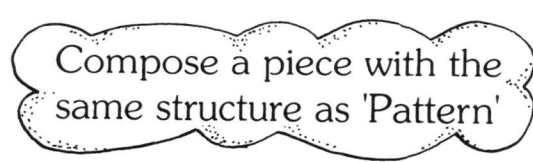

Compose a piece with the same structure as 'Pattern'

Tied notes

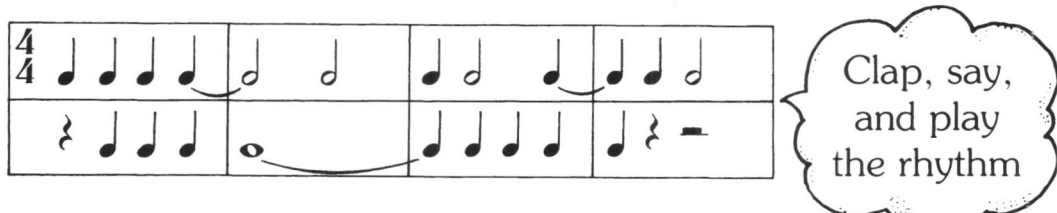

Clap, say, and play the rhythm

A minim tied to a crotchet lasts for 3 beats

A crotchet tied to a crotchet lasts for 2 beats

A semibreve tied to a crotchet lasts for 5 beats, and so on

When the saints go marching in

Old Texas

Syncopation

The rolling heather

Scottish traditional

Moderato

Twelve bar blues

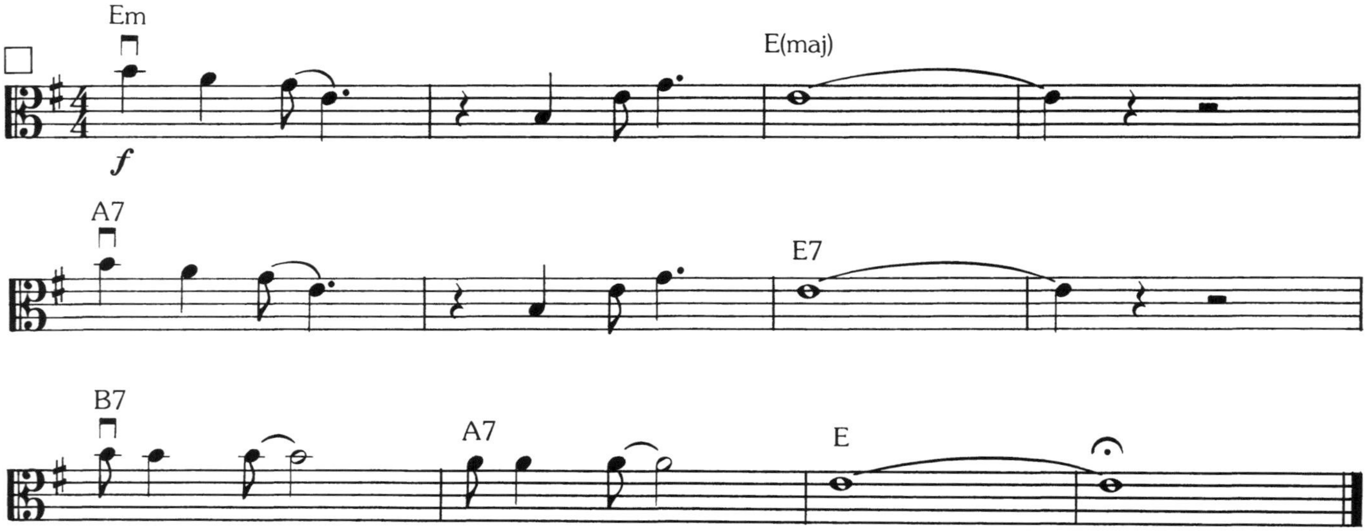

Jamaican dance

Traditional

Sing a rainbow

Words and Music by
ARTHUR HAMILTON

Semplice

Sam's piece

Composed by thirteen-year old Sam Wilkinson

Allegro

The white cliffs of Dover

Words by WALTER KENT
Music by NAT BURTON

Sentimentally

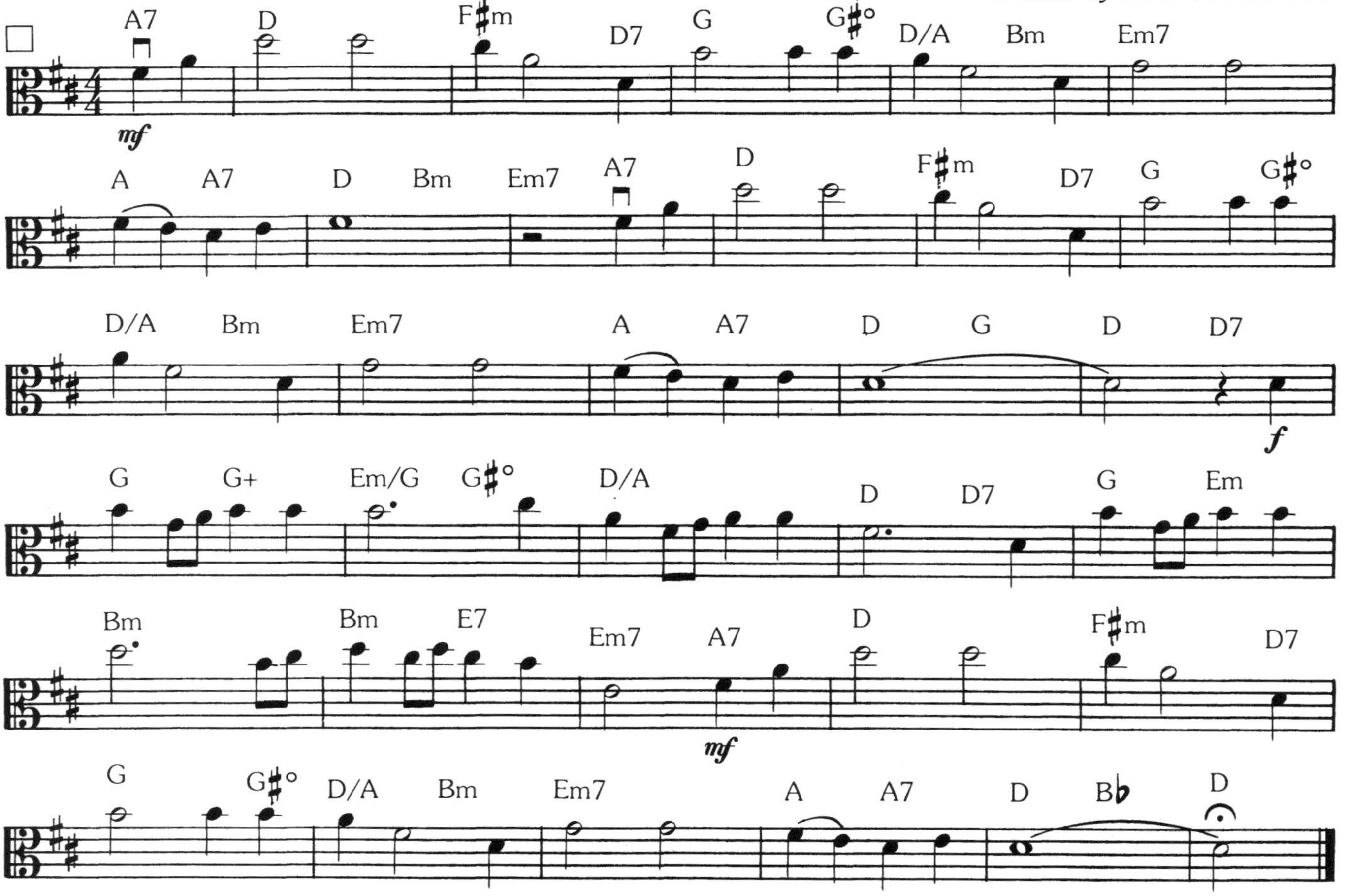

All night, all day

Spiritual

In 5/4 time each bar adds up to five crotchet beats

The clowns

Composed by thirteen-year old Collette Cassidy

I gave my love a cherry

Traditional

Passion chorale

JOHANN SEBASTIAN BACH
(1685-1750)

Old Macdonald

Traditional

The key of G major

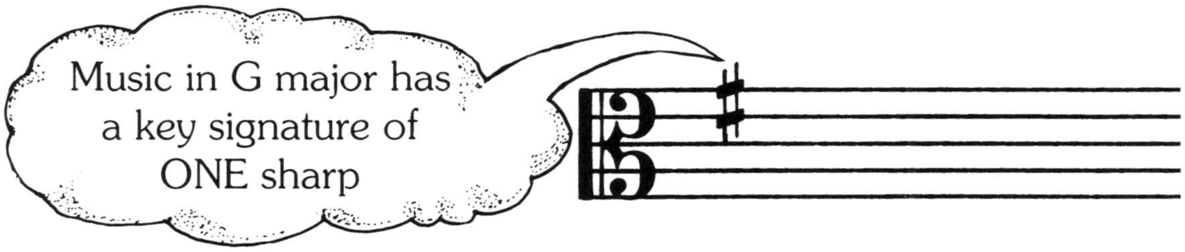

Music in G major has a key signature of ONE sharp

This C is written above one leger line. It is played with '2nd finger back'

2nd finger back

2nd finger forward

Love me tender

Words and Music by
VERA MATSON and ELVIS PRESLEY

Caressingly

2nd finger back

Valse

Yankee Doodle

American traditional

The grand old Duke of York

English traditional

Summer song

Czech traditional

Good King Wenceslas

English traditional carol

1.

2.

3.

$\frac{6}{8}$ time

and its relationship with $\frac{2}{4}$ time.

Semiquavers

Four SEMIQUAVERS (or SIXTEENTH NOTES) add up to one crotchet

Clap, say, and play the rhythm

Semiquaver study

Allegro

Gallop

From the opera *Orpheus in the Underworld*

JACQUES OFFENBACH (1819-1880)

Allegro vivo

Dotted quavers

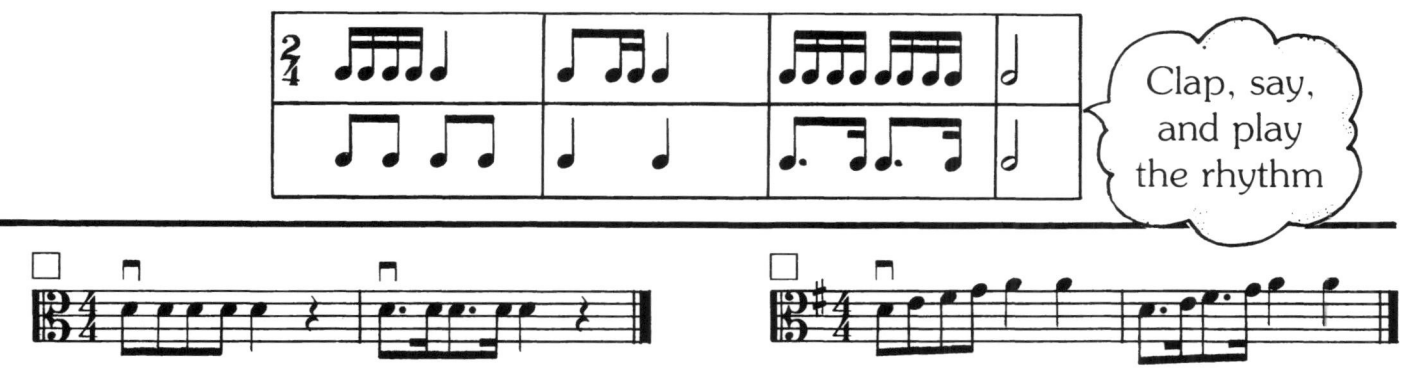

Clap, say, and play the rhythm

Happy birthday to you

Moderato

Words and Music by
PATTY S. HILL and MILDRED HILL

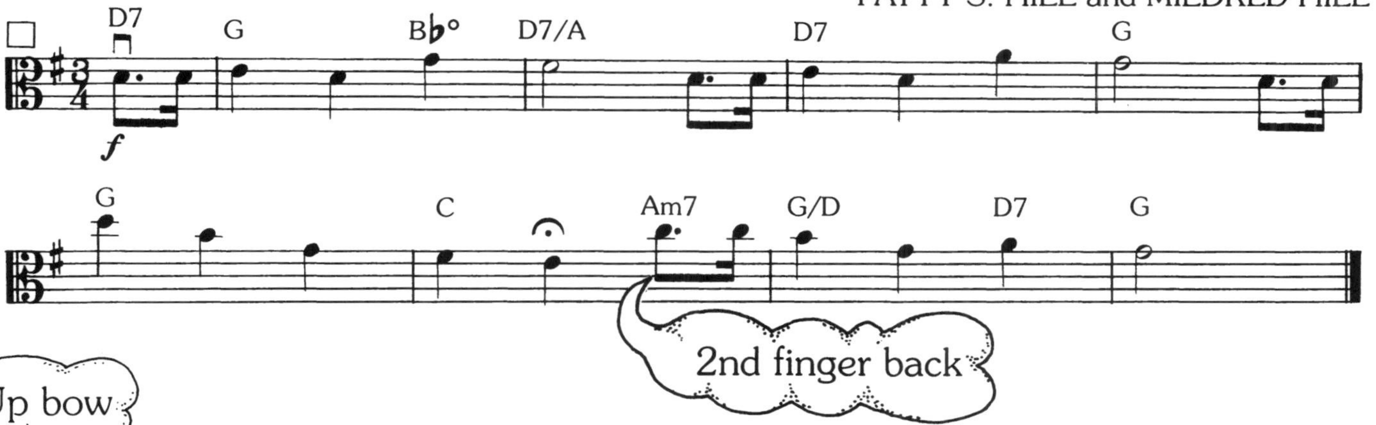

2nd finger back

Up bow

Oh Susannah

American traditional

Brightly

TWO MINIM BEATS in each bar

Chitty Chitty Bang Bang

Words and Music by
RICHARD SHERMAN and ROBERT SHERMAN

Scarboro' fair

Traditional

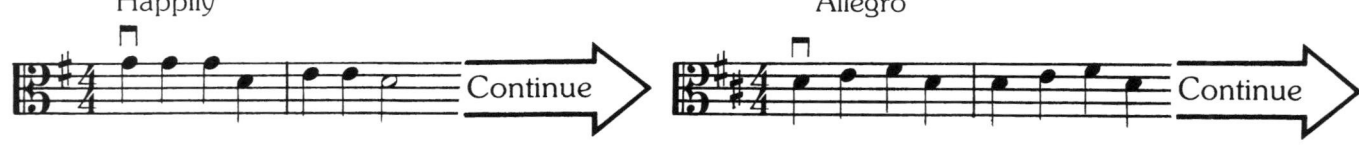

The QUAVER TRIPLET means that three quavers are played in the time of one crotchet

Amazing grace

Traditional

1.

Slowly

mp

3

3

3

2.

Slowly

mp

2nd finger back

3.

Slowly

mp

Slurring three notes to a bow

Ruthin gardens

Tyrolean song

Silent night

FRANZ GRUBER
(1787-1863)

The Skye boat song

Scottish traditional

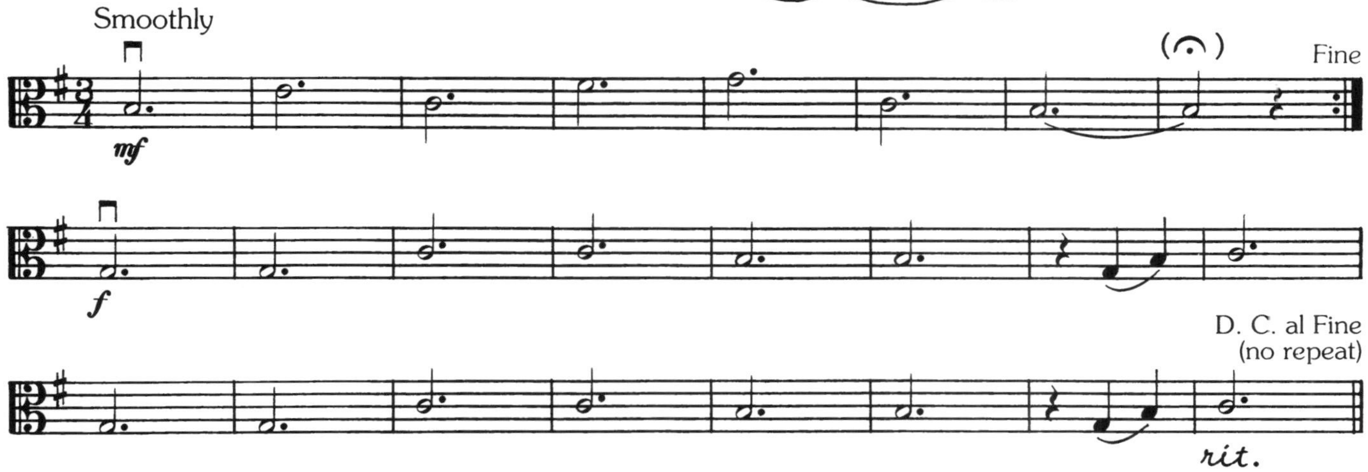

Scales and arpeggios

G major

D major

C major

C major (2 octaves)

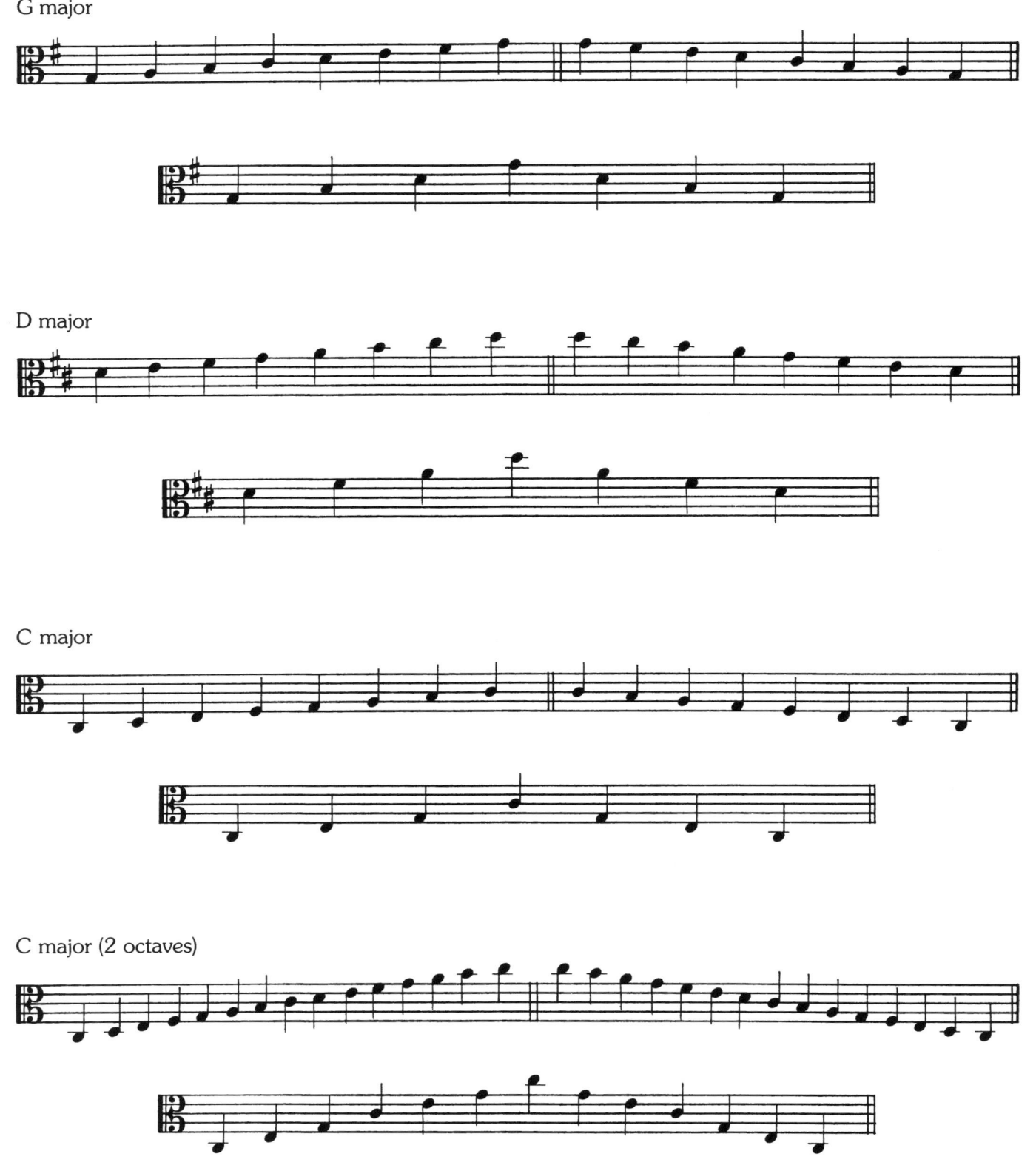